Words to Know Before You Read

chew

clutter

darted

notice

prickly

sandspur

yelping

www.rourkepublishing.com

Edited by Luana K. Mitten
Illustrated by Bob Reese
Art Direction and Page Layout by Renee Brady

Library of Congress Cataloging-in-Publication Data

Picou, Lin
 Puppy Trouble / Lin Picou.
    p. cm. -- (Little Birdie Books)
 ISBN 978-1-61741-814-3 (hard cover) (alk. paper)
 ISBN 978-1-61236-018-8 (soft cover)
 Library of Congress Control Number: 2011924665

Rourke Publishing
Printed in the United States of America, North Mankato, Minnesota
060711
060711CL

www.rourkepublishing.com - rourke@rourkepublishing.com
Post Office Box 643328 Vero Beach, Florida 32964

Puppy Trouble

By Lin Picou

Illustrated by Bob Reese

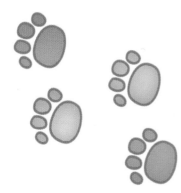

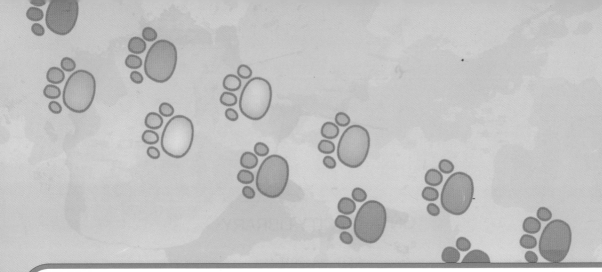

"Mom! Dad! Guess what?"

"What Jake?" Dad asked.

"Molly's puppies are all looking for new homes. Can we have one?" Jake wanted to know.

5

"If we took a puppy, you would have to take it for walks," explained Mom.

Dad added, "Dogs need to take baths, too."

"I could give the dog a bath," Julie said.

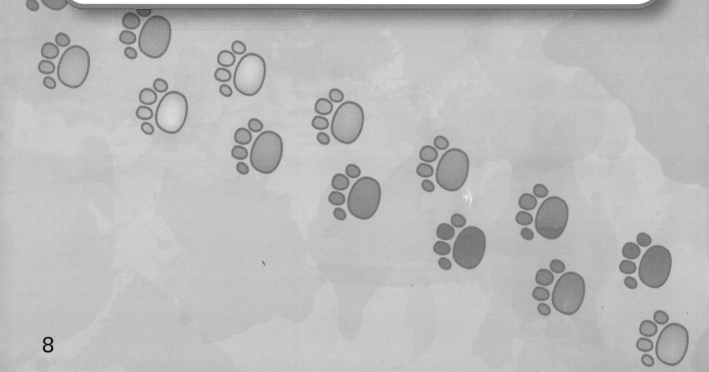

Jake and Julie talked their parents into picking out a puppy. Their new puppy, Tank, was excited about all the new smells, sounds, and clutter.

9

Everything was a chew toy for Tank! "Oh no!" yelled Julie. "Tank has unrolled half the roll of toilet paper."

Jake noticed, "He cleaned out the candy bowl and ate the candy wrappers, too!"

13

She decided to put her shoes outside in the trash so her parents wouldn't see them.

When she opened the door, Tank darted out!

"Jake," Julie yelled, "please help me catch Tank!" They ran after Tank.

Suddenly, Tank stopped running and started yelping. "What's the matter, Tank?" they asked.

Julie took his paw in her hand and found a prickly sandspur. She carefully pulled it out and then carried him inside.

Julie and Jake agreed that a dog may be a man's best friend but a puppy can get into lots of trouble!

21

After Reading Activities

You and the Story...

Why is the book called *Puppy Trouble?*

What trouble did Tank get into?

What are some things you must do to care for a puppy?

Do you have a pet? If so, what are you responsible for? If not, what type of pet would you like? What would you have to do to care for your pet?

Words You Know Now...

Which words can you add an 's' to the ending? Write those words on a piece of paper.

chew	prickly
clutter	sandspur
darted	yelping
notice	

You Could... Make a Poster About Caring for Pets

- Choose a pet.

- Make a list of all the things that need to be done to care for the pet.

- Create a poster telling people how to care for this type of pet. Be sure to illustrate each of the responsibilities.

About the Author

Cats, rabbits, gardening, and reading lots of books are Lin Picou's hobbies. As a child she played school with her sister and then later received her Master's Degree in English Education. Now she teaches and tutors children of all ages in Lutz and Land O' Lakes, Florida.

About the Illustrator ?

Bob Reese began his art career at age 17 working for Walt Disney. His projects included the animated feature films Sleeping Beauty, The Sword and the Stone, and Paul Bunyan. He has also worked for Bob Clampett and Hanna Barbera Studios. He resides in Utah and enjoys spending time with his two daughters, five grandchildren, and cat named Venus.